CHILDREN'S THRIFT CLASSICS

Irish Fairy Tales

Edited by Philip Smith

Illustrated by Thea Kliros

DOVER PUBLICATIONS, INC.
New York

DOVER CHILDREN'S THRIFT CLASSICS
EDITOR: PHILIP SMITH

Published in Canada by General Publishing Company, Ltd., 30 Lesmill Road, Don Mills, Toronto, Ontario.

Published in the United Kingdom by Constable and Company, Ltd., 3 The Lanchesters, 162–164 Fulham Palace Road, London W6 9ER.

Irish Fairy Tales, first published by Dover Publications, Inc., in 1993, is a new anthology containing the unabridged texts of eight works selected from the following: T. Crofton Croker, *Fairy Legends and Traditions of the South of Ireland* (1825–8; "The Giant's Stairs"); Joseph Jacobs (ed.), *Celtic Fairy Tales* (1892 [Dover reprint edition 0-486-21826-0]; "The Sprightly Tailor," "The Field of Boliauns," "Hudden and Dudden and Donald O'Neary") and *More Celtic Fairy Tales* (1894 [Dover reprint edition 0-486-21827-9]; "The Black Horse"); and Seumas MacManus, *Donegal Fairy Stories* (1900 [Dover reprint edition 0-486-21971-2]; "The Bee, the Harp, the Mouse, and the Bum-Clock," "Conal and Donal and Taig," "The Old Hag's Long Leather Bag"). The illustrations and introductory Note have been specially created for this edition, and some explanatory notes have been added.

Manufactured in the United States of America
Dover Publications, Inc., 31 East 2nd Street, Mineola, N.Y. 11501

Library of Congress Cataloging-in-Publication Data

Irish fairy tales / edited by Philip Smith ; illustrated by Thea Kliros.
    p.   cm. — (Dover children's thrift classics)
    Contents: The bee, the harp, the mouse, and the bum-clock — The sprightly tailor — Conal and Donal and Taig — The black horse — The field of Boliauns — Hudden and Dudden and Donald O'Neary — The old hag's long leather bag — The giant's stairs.
    ISBN 0-486-27572-8
    1. Fairy tales—Ireland. 2. Tales—Ireland. [1. Fairy tales. 2. Folklore—Ireland.] I. Kliros, Thea, ill. II. Series.
PZ8.I67 1993
[398.21'09415]—dc20
                                                                93–243
                                                                  CIP
                                                                   AC

Note

The fairy tales of Ireland—told in colorful language, often concerning fanciful creatures and the humans who encounter them—are among the most admired of any land. The stories in this volume represent a sampling of the many varieties of Irish folk tales, from treasure tales concerning "the good people" to amusements celebrating the quick-witted and clever. Each has its own special sound and words, reflecting the unique lilt and dialect of a particular region of Ireland. (Translations have been supplied for some unfamiliar words, for those who require them.)

As you read these stories, keep in mind that many of them were preserved for centuries in spoken form before being written down, and that many persons hearing and telling these tales believed literally in their supernatural subjects.

Contents

List of Illustrations

The Bee, the Harp, the Mouse, and the Bum-Clock

ONCE THERE WAS a widow, and she had one son, called Jack. Jack and his mother owned just three cows. They lived well and happy for a long time; but at last hard times came down on them, and the crops failed, and poverty looked in at the door, and things got so sore against the poor widow that for want of money and for want of necessities she had to make up her mind to sell one of the cows. "Jack," she said one night, "go over in the morning to the fair to sell the branny [speckled brown] cow."

Well and good: in the morning my brave Jack was up early, and took a stick in his fist and turned out the cow, and off to the fair he went with her; and when Jack came into the fair, he saw a great crowd gathered in a ring in the street. He went into the crowd to see what they were looking at, and there in the

1

middle of them he saw a man with a wee, wee harp, a mouse, and a bum-clock [cockroach], and a bee to play the harp. And when the man put them down on the ground and whistled, the bee began to play the harp, and the mouse and the bum-clock stood up on their hind legs and got hold of each other and began to waltz. And as soon as the harp began to play and the mouse and the bum-clock to dance, there wasn't a man or woman, or a thing in the fair, that didn't begin to dance also; and the pots and pans, and the wheels and reels jumped and jigged, all over the town, and Jack himself and the branny cow were as bad as the next.

There was never a town in such a state before or since, and after a while the man picked up the bee, the harp, and the mouse, and the bum-clock and put them into his pocket, and the men and women, Jack and the cow, the pots and pans, wheels and reels, that had hopped and jigged, now stopped, and every one began to laugh as if to break its heart. Then the man turned to Jack. "Jack," says he, "how would you like to be master of all these animals?"

"Why," says Jack, "I should like it fine."

"Well, then," says the man, "how will you and me make a bargain about them?"

"I have no money," says Jack.

The bee began to play the harp, and the
mouse and the bum-clock stood up on their
hind legs and began to waltz.

"But you have a fine cow," says the man. "I will give you the bee and the harp for it."

"O, but," Jack says, says he, "my poor mother at home is very sad and sorrowful entirely, and I have this cow to sell and lift her heart again."

"And better than this she cannot get," says the man. "For when she sees the bee play the harp, she will laugh if she never laughed in her life before."

"Well," says Jack, says he, "that will be grand."

He made the bargain. The man took the cow; and Jack started home with the bee and the harp in his pocket, and when he came home, his mother welcomed him back.

"And Jack," says she, "I see you have sold the cow."

"I have done that," says Jack.

"Did you do well?" says the mother.

"I did well, and very well," says Jack.

"How much did you get for her?" says the mother.

"O," says he, "it was not for money at all I sold her, but for something far better."

"O, Jack! Jack!" says she, "what have you done?"

"Just wait until you see, mother," says he, "and you will soon say I have done well."

Out of his pocket he takes the bee and the

harp and sets them in the middle of the floor, and whistles to them, and as soon as he did this the bee began to play the harp, and the mother she looked at them and let a big, great laugh out of her, and she and Jack began to dance, the pots and pans, the wheels and reels began to jig and dance over the floor, and the house itself hopped about also.

When Jack picked up the bee and the harp again the dancing all stopped, and the mother laughed for a long time. But when she came to herself, she got very angry entirely with Jack, and she told him he was a silly, foolish fellow, that there was neither food nor money in the house, and now he had lost one of her good cows also. "We must do something to live," says she. "Over to the fair you must go to-morrow morning, and take the black cow with you and sell her."

And off in the morning at an early hour brave Jack started, and never halted until he was in the fair. When he came into the fair, he saw a big crowd gathered in a ring in the street. Said Jack to himself, "I wonder what are they looking at."

Into the crowd he pushed, and saw the wee man this day again with a mouse and a bum-clock, and he put them down in the street and whistled. The mouse and the bum-clock stood up on their hind legs and got hold of each other and began to dance there and jig, and as they did there was not a man or woman in the street who didn't begin to jig also, and Jack and the black cow, and the wheels and the reels, and the pots and pans, all of them were jigging and dancing all over the town, and the houses themselves were jumping and hopping about, and such a place Jack or any one else never saw before.

When the man lifted the mouse and the bum-clock into his pocket, they all stopped dancing and settled down, and everybody laughed right hearty. The man turned to Jack. "Jack," said he, "I am glad to see you; how would you like to have these animals?"

"I should like well to have them," says Jack, says he, "only I cannot."

"Why cannot you?" says the man.

"O," says Jack, says he, "I have no money, and my poor mother is very down-hearted. She sent me to the fair to sell this cow and bring some money to lift her heart."

"O," says the man, says he, "if you want to lift your mother's heart I will sell you the mouse, and when you set the bee to play the harp and the mouse to dance to it, your mother will laugh if she never laughed in her life before."

"But I have no money," says Jack, says he, "to buy your mouse."

"I don't mind," says the man, says he, "I will take your cow for it."

Poor Jack was so taken with the mouse and had his mind so set on it, that he thought it was a grand bargain entirely, and he gave the man his cow, and took the mouse and started off for home, and when he got home his mother welcomed him.

"Jack," says she, "I see you have sold the cow."

"I did that," says Jack.

"Did you sell her well?" says she.

"Very well indeed," says Jack, says he.

"How much did you get for her?"

"I didn't get money," says he, "but I got value."

"O, Jack! Jack!" says she, "what do you mean?"

"I will soon show you that, mother," says he, taking the mouse out of his pocket and the harp and the bee and setting all on the floor; and when he began to whistle the bee began to play, and the mouse got up on its hind legs and began to dance and jig, and the mother gave such a hearty laugh as she never laughed in her life before. To dancing and jigging herself and Jack fell, and the pots and pans and the wheels and reels began to dance and jig over the floor, and the house jigged also. And when they were tired of this, Jack lifted the harp and the mouse and the bee and put them in his pocket, and his mother she laughed for a long time.

But when she got over that she got very down-hearted and very angry entirely with Jack. "And O, Jack," she says, "you are a stupid, good-for-nothing fellow. We have neither money nor meat in the house, and here you have lost two of my good cows, and I have only one left now. To-morrow morning," she says, "you must be up early and take this cow to the fair and sell her. See to get something to lift my heart up."

"I will do that," says Jack, says he. So he went to his bed, and early in the morning he was up and turned out the spotty cow and went to the fair.

When Jack got to the fair, he saw a crowd gathered in a ring in the street. "I wonder what they are looking at, anyhow," says he. He pushed through the crowd, and there he saw the same wee man he had seen before, with a bum-clock; and when he put the bum-clock on the ground, he whistled, and the bum-clock began to dance, and the men, women, and children in the street, and Jack and the spotty cow began to dance and jig also, and everything on the street and about it, the wheels and reels, the pots and pans, began to jig, and the houses themselves began to dance likewise. And when the man lifted the bum-clock and put it in his pocket, everybody stopped jigging and dancing and every one laughed loud. The wee man turned, and saw Jack.

"Jack, my brave boy," says he, "you will never be right fixed until you have this bum-clock, for it is a very fancy thing to have."

"O, but," says Jack, says he, "I have no money."

"No matter for that," says the man; "you have a cow, and that is as good as money to me."

"Well," says Jack, "I have a poor mother who is very down-hearted at home, and she sent me to the fair to sell this cow and raise some money and lift her heart."

"O, but Jack," says the wee man, "this bum-clock is the very thing to lift her heart, for when you put down your harp and bee and mouse on the floor, and put the bum-clock along with them, she will laugh if she never laughed in her life before."

"Well, that is surely true," says Jack, says he, "and I think I will make a swap with you."

So Jack gave the cow to the man and took the bum-clock himself, and started for home.

His mother was glad to see Jack back, and says she, "Jack, I see that you have sold the cow."

"I did that, mother," says Jack.

"Did you sell her well, Jack?" says the mother.

"Very well indeed, mother," says Jack.

"How much did you get for her?" says the mother.

"I didn't take any money for her, mother, but value," says Jack, and he takes out of his pocket the bum-clock and the mouse, and set them on the floor and began to whistle, and the bee began to play the harp and the mouse and the bum-clock stood up on their hind legs and began to dance, and Jack's mother laughed very hearty, and everything in the house, the wheels and the reels, and the pots and pans, went jigging and hopping over the floor, and the house itself went jigging and hopping about likewise.

When Jack lifted up the animals and put them in his pocket, everything stopped, and the mother laughed for a good while. But after a while, when she came to herself, and saw what Jack had done and how they were now without either money, or food, or a cow, she got very, very angry at Jack, and scolded him hard, and then sat down and began to cry.

Poor Jack, when he looked at himself, confessed that he was a stupid fool entirely. "And what," says he, "shall I now do for my poor mother?" He went out along the road, thinking and thinking, and he met a wee woman who said, "Good-morrow to you. Jack," says she, "how is it you are not trying for the King's daughter of Ireland?"

"What do you mean?" says Jack.

Says she: "Didn't you hear what the whole world has heard, that the King of Ireland has a daughter who hasn't laughed for seven years, and he has promised to give her in marriage, and to give the kingdom along with her, to any man who will take three laughs out of her."

"If that is so," says Jack, says he, "it is not here I should be."

Back to the house he went, and gathers together the bee, the harp, the mouse, and the bum-clock, and putting them into his pocket, he bade his mother good-by, and told her it wouldn't be long till she got good news from him, and off he hurries.

When he reached the castle, there was a ring of spikes all round the castle and men's heads on nearly every spike there.

"What heads are these?" Jack asked one of the King's soldiers.

"Any man that comes here trying to win the

King's daughter, and fails to make her laugh three times, loses his head and has it stuck on a spike. These are the heads of the men that failed," says he.

"A mighty big crowd," says Jack, says he. Then Jack sent word to tell the King's daughter and the King that there was a new man who had come to win her.

In a very little time the King and the King's daughter and the King's court all came out and sat themselves down on gold and silver chairs in front of the castle, and ordered Jack to be brought in until he should have his trial. Jack, before he went, took out of his pocket the bee, the harp, the mouse, and the bumclock, and he gave the harp to the bee, and he tied a string to one and the other, and took the end of the string himself, and marched into the castle yard before all the court, with his animals coming on a string behind him.

When the Queen and the King and the court and the princes saw poor ragged Jack with his bee, and mouse, and bum-clock hopping behind him on a string, they set up one roar of laughter that was long and loud enough, and when the King's daughter herself lifted her head and looked to see what they were laughing at, and saw Jack and his paraphernalia, she opened her mouth and she let out of her such a laugh as was never heard before.

Then Jack dropped a low courtesy, and said, "Thank you, my lady; I have one of the three parts of you won."

Then he drew up his animals in a circle, and began to whistle, and the minute he did, the bee began to play the harp, and the mouse and the bum-clock stood up on their hind legs, got hold of each other, and began to dance, and the King and the King's court and Jack himself began to dance and jig, and everything about the King's castle, pots and pans, wheels and reels and the castle itself began to dance also. And the King's daughter, when she saw this, opened her mouth again, and let out of her a laugh twice louder than she let before, and Jack, in the middle of his jigging, drops another courtesy, and says, "Thank you, my lady; that is two of the three parts of you won."

Jack and his menagerie went on playing and dancing, but Jack could not get the third laugh out of the King's daughter, and the poor fellow saw his big head in danger of going on the spike. Then the brave mouse came to Jack's help and wheeled round upon its heel, and as it did so its tail swiped into the bum-clock's mouth, and the bum-clock began to cough and cough and cough. And when the King's daughter saw this she opened her mouth again, and she let the loudest and hard-

est and merriest laugh that was ever heard
before or since; and, "Thank you, my lady,"
says Jack, dropping another courtesy; "I have
all of you won."

Then when Jack stopped his menagerie, the
King took himself and the menagerie within
the castle. He was washed and combed, and
dressed in a suit of silk and satin, with all
kinds of gold and silver ornaments, and then
was led before the King's daughter. And true
enough she confessed that a handsomer and
finer fellow than Jack she had never seen, and
she was very willing to be his wife.

Jack sent for his poor old mother and
brought her to the wedding, which lasted nine
days and nine nights, every night better than
the other. All the lords and ladies and gentry
of Ireland were at the wedding. I was at it,
too, and got brogues, broth and slippers of
bread and came jigging home on my head.

The Sprightly Tailor

A SPRIGHTLY TAILOR was employed by the great Macdonald, in his castle at Saddell, in order to make the laird a pair of trews, used in olden time. And trews being the vest and breeches united in one piece, and ornamented with fringes, were very comfortable, and suitable to be worn in walking or dancing. And Macdonald had said to the tailor, that if he would make the trews by night in the church, he would get a handsome reward. For it was thought that the old ruined church was haunted, and that fearsome things were to be seen there at night.

The tailor was well aware of this; but he was a sprightly man, and when the laird dared him to make the trews by night in the church, the tailor was not to be daunted, but took it in hand to gain the prize. So, when night came, away he went up the glen, about half a mile distance from the castle, till he came to the old church. Then he chose him a nice grave-stone for a seat and he lighted his candle, and put on his thimble, and set to work at the trews; plying his needle nimbly, and thinking about the hire [pay] that the laird would have to give him.

For some time he got on pretty well, until he felt the floor all of a tremble under his feet; and looking about him, but keeping his fingers at work, he saw the appearance of a great human head rising up through the stone pavement of the church. And when the head had risen above the surface, there came from it a great, great voice. And the voice said: "Do you see this great head of mine?"

"I see that, but I'll sew this!" replied the sprightly tailor; and he stitched away at the trews.

Then the head rose higher up through the pavement, until its neck appeared. And when its neck was shown, the thundering voice came again and said: "Do you see this great neck of mine?"

"I see that, but I'll sew this!" said the sprightly tailor; and he stitched away at his trews.

Then the head and neck rose higher still, until the great shoulders and chest were shown above the ground. And again the mighty voice thundered: "Do you see this great chest of mine?"

"Do you see this great chest of mine?"

And again the sprightly tailor replied: "I see that, but I'll sew this!" and stitched away at his trews.

And still it kept rising through the pavement, until it shook a great pair of arms in the tailor's face, and said: "Do you see these great arms of mine?"

"I see those, but I'll sew this!" answered the tailor; and he stitched hard at his trews, for he knew that he had no time to lose.

The sprightly tailor was taking the long stitches, when he saw it gradually rising and rising through the floor, until it lifted out a great leg, and stamping with it upon the pavement, said in a roaring voice: "Do you see this great leg of mine?"

"Aye, aye: I see that, but I'll sew this!" cried the tailor; and his fingers flew with the needle, and he took such long stitches, that he was just come to the end of the trews, when it was taking up its other leg. But before it could pull it out of the pavement, the sprightly tailor had finished his task; and, blowing out his candle, and springing from off his gravestone, he buckled up, and ran out of the church with the trews under his arm. Then the fearsome thing gave a loud roar, and stamped with both his feet upon the pavement, and out of the church he went after the sprightly tailor.

Down the glen they ran, faster than the
stream when the flood rides it; but the tailor
had got the start and a nimble pair of legs,
and he did not choose to lose the laird's
reward. And though the thing roared to him to
stop, yet the sprightly tailor was not the man
to be beholden to a monster. So he held his
trews tight, and let no darkness grow under
his feet, until he had reached Saddell Castle.
He had no sooner got inside the gate, and shut
it, than the apparition came up to it; and,
enraged at losing his prize, struck the wall
above the gate, and left there the mark of his
five great fingers. Ye may see them plainly to
this day, if ye'll only peer close enough.

But the sprightly tailor gained his reward:
for Macdonald paid him handsomely for the
trews, and never discovered that a few of the
stitches were somewhat long.

Conal and Donal and Taig

ONCE THERE WERE three brothers named Conal, Donal and Taig, and they fell out regarding which of them owned a field of land. One of them had as good a claim to it as the other, and the claims of all of them were so equal that none of the judges, whomsoever they went before, could decide in favor of one more than the other.

At length they went to one judge who was very wise indeed and had a great name, and every one of them stated his case to him.

He sat on the bench, and heard Conal's case and Donal's case and Taig's case all through, with very great patience. When the three of them had finished, he said he would take a day and a night to think it all over, and on the day after, when they were all called into court again, the Judge said that he had weighed the evidence on all sides, with all the deliberation

21

it was possible to give it, and he decided that
one of them hadn't the shadow of a shade of a
claim more than the others, so that he found
himself facing the greatest puzzle he had ever
faced in his life.

"But," says he, "no puzzle puzzles me long.
I'll very soon decide which of you will get the
field. You seem to me to be three pretty lazy-
looking fellows, and I'll give the field to
whichever of the three of you is the laziest."

"Well, at that rate," says Conal, "it's me gets
the field, for I'm the laziest man of the lot."

"How lazy are you?" says the Judge.

"Well," said Conal, "if I were lying in the
middle of the road, and there was a regiment
of troopers come galloping down it, I'd sooner
let them ride over me than take the bother of
getting up and going to the one side."

"Well, well," says the Judge, says he, "you
are a lazy man surely, and I doubt if Donal or
Taig can be as lazy as that."

"Oh, faith," says Donal, "I'm just every bit as
lazy."

"Are you?" says the Judge. "How lazy are
you?"

"Well," said Donal, "if I was sitting right
close to a big fire, and you piled on it all the
turf in a townland and all the wood in a barony, sooner than have to move I'd sit there till

the boiling marrow would run out of my bones."

"Well," says the Judge, "you're a pretty lazy man, Donal, and I doubt if Taig is as lazy as either of you."

"Indeed, then," says Taig, "I'm every bit as lazy."

"How can that be?" says the Judge.

"Well," says Taig, "if I was lying on the broad of my back in the middle of the floor and looking up at the rafters, and if soot drops were falling as thick as hailstones from the rafters into my open eyes, I would let them drop there for the length of the lee-long [livelong] day sooner than take the bother of closing the eyes."

"Well," says the Judge, "that's very wonderful entirely, and," says he, "I'm in as great a quandary as before, for I see you are the three laziest men that ever were known since the world began, and which of you is the laziest it certainly beats me to say. But I'll tell you what I'll do," says the Judge, "I'll give the field to the oldest man of you."

"Then," says Conal, "it's me gets the field."

"How is that?" says the Judge; "how old are you?"

"Well, I'm that old," says Conal, "that when I was twenty-one years of age I got a shipload of awls and never lost nor broke one of them, and I wore out the last of them yesterday mending my shoes."

"Well, well," says the Judge, says he, "you're surely an old man, and I doubt very much that Donal and Taig can catch up to you."

"Can't I?" says Donal; "take care of that."

"Why," said the Judge, "how old are you?"

"When I was twenty-one years of age," says Donal, "I got a shipload of needles, and yesterday I wore out the last of them mending my clothes."

"Well, well, well," says the Judge, says he, "you're two very, very old men, to be sure, and I'm afraid poor Taig is out of his chance anyhow."

"Take care of that," says Taig.

"Why," said the Judge, "how old are you, Taig?"

Says Taig, "When I was twenty-one years of age I got a shipload of razors, and yesterday I had the last of them worn to a stump shaving myself."

"Well," says the Judge, says he, "I've often heard tell of old men," he says, "but anything as old as what you three are never was known since Methusalem's cat died. The like of your ages," he says, "I never heard tell of, and which of you is the oldest, that surely beats me to decide, and I'm in a quandary again. But

I'll tell you what I'll do," says the Judge, says he, "I'll give the field to whichever of you minds [remembers] the longest."

"Well, if that's it," says Conal, "it's me gets the field, for I mind the time when if a man tramped on a cat he usen't to give it a kick to console it."

"Well, well, well," says the Judge, "that must be a long mind entirely; and I'm afraid, Conal, you have the field."

"Not so quick," says Donal, says he, "for I mind the time when a woman wouldn't speak an ill word of her best friend."

"Well, well, well," says the Judge, "your memory, Donal, must certainly be a very wonderful one, if you can mind that time. Taig," says the Judge, says he, "I'm afraid your memory can't compare with Conal's and Donal's."

"Can't it," says Taig, says he. "Take care of that, for I mind the time when you wouldn't find nine liars in a crowd of ten men."

"Oh, Oh, Oh!" says the Judge, says he, "that memory of yours, Taig, must be a wonderful one." Says he: "Such memories as you three men have were never known before, and which of you has the greatest memory it beats me to say. But I'll tell you what I'll do now," says he; "I'll give the field to whichever of you has the keenest sight."

"Then," says Conal, says he, "it's me gets the field; because," says he, "if there was a fly perched on the top of yon mountain, ten miles away, I could tell you every time he blinked."

"You have wonderful sight, Conal," says the Judge, says he, "and I'm afraid you've got the field."

"Take care," says Donal, says he, "but I've got as good. For I could tell you whether it was a mote in his eye that made him blink or not."

"Ah, ha, ha!" says the Judge, says he, "this is wonderful sight surely. Taig," says he, "I pity you, for you have no chance for the field now."

"Have I not?" says Taig. "I could tell you from here whether that fly was in good health or not by counting his heart beats."

"Well, well, well," says the Judge, says he, "I'm in as great a quandary as ever. You are three of the most wonderful men that ever I met, and no mistake. But I'll tell you what I'll do," says he; "I'll give the field to the supplest man of you."

"Thank you," says Conal. "Then the field is mine."

"Why so?" says the Judge.

"Because," says Conal, says he, "if you filled that field with hares, and put a dog in the middle of them, and then tied one of my legs up my back, I would not let one of the hares get out."

"Then, Conal," says the Judge, says he, "I think the field is yours."

"By the leave of your judgeship, not yet," says Donal.

"Why, Donal," says the Judge, says he, "surely you are not as supple as that?"

"Am I not?" says Donal. "Do you see that old castle over there without door, or window, or roof in it, and the wind blowing in and out through it like an iron gate?"

"I do," says the Judge. "What about that?"

"Well," says Donal, says he, "if on the stormiest day of the year you had that castle filled with feathers, I would not let a feather be lost, or go ten yards from the castle until I had caught and put it in again."

"Well, surely," says the Judge, says he, "you are a supple man, Donal, and no mistake. Taig," says he, "there's no chance for you now."

"Don't be too sure," says Taig, says he.

"Why," says the Judge, "you couldn't surely do anything to equal these things, Taig?"

Says Taig, says he: "I can shoe the swiftest race-horse in the land when he is galloping at his topmost speed, by driving a nail every time he lifts his foot."

"Well, well, well," says the Judge, says he, "surely you are the three most wonderful men that ever I did meet. The likes of you never was known before, and I suppose the likes of you will never be on the earth again. There is only one other trial," says he, "and if this doesn't decide, I'll have to give it up. I'll give the field, says he, "to the cleverest man amongst you."

"Then," says Conal, says he, "you may as well give it to me at once."

"Why? Are you that clever, Conal?" says the Judge, says he.

"I am that clever," says Conal, "I am that clever, that I would make a skin-fit suit of clothes for a man without any more measurement than to tell me the color of his hair."

"Then, boys," says the Judge, says he, "I think the case is decided."

"Not so quick, my friend," says Donal, "not so quick."

"Why, Donal," says the Judge, says he, "you are surely not cleverer than that?"

"Am I not?" says Donal.

"Why," says the Judge, says he, "what can you do, Donal?"

"Why," says Donal, says he, "I would make a skin-fit suit for a man and give me no more measurement than let me hear him cough."

"Well, well, well," says the Judge, says he, "the cleverness of you two boys beats all I ever heard of. Taig," says he, "poor Taig, whatever chance either of these two may have for the field, I'm very, very sorry for you, for you have no chance."

"Don't be so very sure of that," says Taig, says he.

"Why," says the Judge, says he, "surely, Taig, you can't be as clever as either of them. How clever are you, Taig?"

"Well," says Taig, says he, "if I was a judge, and too stupid to decide a case that came up before me, I'd be that clever that I'd look wise and give some decision."

"Taig," says the Judge, says he, "I've gone into this case and deliberated upon it, and by all the laws of right and justice, I find and decide that you get the field."

The Black Horse

ONCE THERE WAS a king and he had three sons, and when the king died, they did not give a shade of anything to the youngest son, but an old white limping garron [small workhorse].

"If I get but this," quoth he, "it seems that I had best go with this same."

He was going with it right before him, sometimes walking, sometimes riding. When he had been riding a good while he thought that the garron would need a while of eating, so he came down to earth, and what should he see coming out of the heart of the western airt [direction] towards him but a rider riding high, well, and right well.

"All hail, my lad," said he.

"Hail, king's son," said the other.

"What's your news?" said the king's son.

"I have got that," said the lad who came. "I am after breaking my heart riding this ass of a

31

horse; but will you give me the limping white garron for him?"

"No," said the prince; "it would be a bad business for me."

"You need not fear," said the man that came, "there is no saying but that you might make better use of him than I. He has one value, there is no single place that you can think of in the four parts of the wheel of the world that the black horse will not take you there."

So the king's son got the black horse, and he gave the limping white garron.

Where should he think of being when he mounted but in the Realm Underwaves. He went, and before sunrise on the morrow he was there. What should he find when he got there but the son of the King Underwaves holding a Court, and the people of the realm gathered to see if there was any one who would undertake to go to seek the daughter of the King of the Greeks to be the prince's wife. No one came forward, when who should come up but the rider of the black horse.

"You, rider of the black horse," said the prince, "I lay you under crosses and under spells to have the daughter of the King of the Greeks here before the sun rises to-morrow."

He went out and he reached the black horse and leaned his elbow on his mane, and he heaved a sigh.

"Sigh of a king's son under spells!" said the horse; "but have no care; we shall do the thing that was set before you." And so off they went.

"Now," said the horse, "when we get near the great town of the Greeks, you will notice that the four feet of a horse never went to the town before. The king's daughter will see me from the top of the castle looking out of a window, and she will not be content without a turn of a ride upon me. Say that she may have that, but the horse will suffer no man but you to ride before a woman on him."

They came near the big town, and he fell to horsemanship; and the princess was looking out of the windows, and noticed the horse. The horsemanship pleased her, and she came out just as the horse had come.

"Give me a ride on the horse," said she.

"You shall have that," said he, "but the horse will let no man ride him before a woman but me."

"I have a horseman of my own," said she.

"If so, set him in front," said he.

Before the horseman mounted at all, when he tried to get up, the horse lifted his legs and kicked him off.

"Come then yourself and mount before me," said she; "I won't leave the matter so."

He mounted the horse and she behind him,

**Before she glanced from her she was nearer
sky than earth.**

and before she glanced from her she was nearer sky than earth. He was in Realm Underwaves with her before sunrise.

"You are come," said Prince Underwaves.

"I am come," said he.

"There you are, my hero," said the prince. "You are the son of a king, but I am a son of success. Anyhow, we shall have no delay or neglect now, but a wedding."

"Just gently," said the princess; "your wedding is not so short a way off as you suppose. Till I get the silver cup that my grandmother had at her wedding, and that my mother had as well, I will not marry, for I need to have it at my own wedding."

"You, rider of the black horse," said the Prince Underwaves, "I set you under spells and under crosses unless the silver cup is here before dawn to-morrow."

Out he went and reached the horse and leaned his elbow on his mane, and he heaved a sigh.

"Sigh of a king's son under spells!" said the horse; "mount and you shall get the silver cup. The people of the realm are gathered about the king to-night, for he has missed his daughter, and when you get to the palace go in and leave me without; they will have the cup there going round the company. Go in and sit in

their midst. Say nothing, and seem to be as
one of the people of the place. But when the
cup comes round to you, take it under your
oxter [arm], and come out to me with it, and
we'll go."

Away they went and they got to Greece, and
he went in to the palace and did as the black
horse bade. He took the cup and came out
and mounted, and before sunrise he was in
the Realm Underwaves.

"You are come," said Prince Underwaves.

"I am come," said he.

"We had better get married now," said the
prince to the Greek princess.

"Slowly and softly," said she. "I will not
marry till I get the silver ring that my grandmother and my mother wore when they were
wedded."

"You, rider of the black horse," said the
Prince Underwaves, "do that. Let's have that
ring here to-morrow at sunrise."

The lad went to the black horse and put his
elbow on his crest and told him how it was.

"There never was a matter set before me
harder than this matter which has now been
set in front of me," said the horse, "but there
is no help for it at any rate. Mount me. There
is a snow mountain and an ice mountain and a
mountain of fire between us and the winning

of that ring. It is right hard for us to pass them."

Thus they went as they were, and about a mile from the snow mountain they were in a bad case with cold. As they came near it he struck the horse, and with the bound he gave the black horse was on the top of the snow mountain; at the next bound he was on the top of the ice mountain; at the third bound he went through the mountain of fire. When he had passed the mountains he was dragging at the horse's neck, as though he were about to lose himself. He went on before him down to a town below.

"Go down," said the black horse, "to a smithy; make an iron spike for every bone end in me."

Down he went as the horse desired, and he got the spikes made, and back he came with them.

"Stick them into me," said the horse, "every spike of them in every bone end that I have."

That he did; he stuck the spikes into the horse.

"There is a loch here," said the horse, "four miles long and four miles wide, and when I go out into it the loch will take fire and blaze. If you see the Loch of Fire going out before the sun rises, expect me, and if not, go your way."

Out went the black horse into the lake, and
the lake became flame. Long was he stretched
about the lake, beating his palms and roaring.
Day came, and the loch did not go out.

But at the hour when the sun was rising out
of the water the lake went out.

And the black horse rose in the middle of
the water with one single spike in him, and
the ring upon its end.

He came on shore, and down he fell beside
the loch.

Then down went the rider. He got the ring,
and he dragged the horse down to the side of
a hill. He fell to sheltering him with his arms
about him, and as the sun was rising he got
better and better, till about midday, when he
rose on his feet.

"Mount," said the horse, "and let us
begone."

He mounted on the black horse, and away
they went.

He reached the mountains, and he leaped
the horse at the fire mountain and was on the
top. From the mountain of fire he leaped to
the mountain of ice, and from the mountain of
ice to the mountain of snow. He put the
mountains past him, and by morning he was
in realm under the waves.

"You are come," said the prince.

"I am," said he.

"That's true," said Prince Underwaves. "A
king's son are you, but a son of success am I.
We shall have no more mistakes and delays,
but a wedding this time."

"Go easy," said the Princess of the Greeks.
"Your wedding is not so near as you think yet.
Till you make a castle, I won't marry you. Not
to your father's castle nor to your mother's
will I go to dwell; but make me a castle for
which your father's castle will not make
washing water."

"You, rider of the black horse, make that,"
said Prince Underwaves, "before the morrow's sun rises."

The lad went out to the horse and leaned
his elbow on his neck and sighed, thinking
that this castle never could be made for ever.

"There never came a turn in my road yet
that is easier for me to pass than this," said
the black horse.

Glance that the lad gave from him he saw
all that there were, and ever so many wrights
and stone masons at work, and the castle was
ready before the sun rose.

He shouted at the Prince Underwaves, and
he saw the castle. He tried to pluck out his
eye, thinking that it was a false sight.

"Son of King Underwaves," said the rider of
the black horse, "don't think that you have a
false sight; this is a true sight."

"That's true," said the prince. "You are a son of success, but I am a son of success too. There will be no more mistakes and delays, but a wedding now."

"No," said she. "The time is come. Should we not go to look at the castle? There's time enough to get married before the night comes."

They went to the castle and the castle was without a "but" ——

"I see one," said the prince. "One want at least to be made good. A well to be made inside, so that water may not be far to fetch when there is a feast or a wedding in the castle."

"That won't be long undone," said the rider of the black horse.

The well was made, and it was seven fathoms deep and two or three fathoms wide, and they looked at the well on the way to the wedding.

"It is very well made," said she, "but for one little fault yonder."

"Where is it?" said Prince Underwaves.

"There," said she.

He bent him down to look. She came out, and she put her two hands at his back, and cast him in.

"Be thou there," said she. "If I go to be married, thou art not the man; but the man who did each exploit that has been done, and, if he chooses, him will I have."

Away she went with the rider of the little black horse to the wedding.

And at the end of three years after that so it was that he first remembered the black horse or where he left him.

He got up and went out, and he was very sorry for his neglect of the black horse. He found him just where he left him.

"Good luck to you, gentleman," said the horse. "You seem as if you had got something that you like better than me."

"I have not got that, and I won't; but it came over me to forget you," said he.

"I don't mind," said the horse, "it will make no difference. Raise your sword and smite off my head."

"Fortune will now allow that I should do that," said he.

"Do it instantly, or I will do it to you," said the horse.

So the lad drew his sword and smote off the horse's head; then he lifted his two palms and uttered a doleful cry.

What should he hear behind him but "All hail, my brother-in-law."

He looked behind him, and there was the finest man he ever set eyes upon.

"What set you weeping for the black horse?" said he.

"This," said the lad, "that there never was born of man or beast a creature in this world that I was fonder of."

"Would you take me for him?" said the stranger.

"If I could think you the horse, I would; but if not, I would rather the horse," said the rider.

"I am the black horse," said the lad, "and if I were not, how should you have all these things that you went to seek in my father's house. Since I went under spells, many a man have I ran at before you met me. They had but one word amongst them: they could not keep me, nor manage me, and they never kept me a couple of days. But when I fell in with you, you kept me till the time ran out that was to come from the spells. And now you shall go home with me, and we will make a wedding in my father's house."

The Field of Boliauns

ONE FINE DAY in harvest—it was indeed Lady-day in harvest, that everybody knows to be one of the greatest holidays in the year—Tom Fitzpatrick was taking a ramble through the ground, and went along the sunny side of a hedge; when all of a sudden he heard a clacking sort of noise a little before him in the hedge. "Dear me," said Tom, "but isn't it surprising to hear the stonechatters singing so late in the season?" So Tom stole on, going on the tops of his toes to try if he could get a sight of what was making the noise, to see if he was right in his guess. The noise stopped; but as Tom looked sharply through the bushes, what should he see in a nook of the hedge but a brown pitcher, that might hold about a gallon and a half of liquor; and by-and-by a little wee teeny tiny bit of an old man, with a little *motty* of a cocked hat stuck upon the top of his head, a deeshy

"God bless your work, neighbour," said Tom.

daushy leather apron hanging before him, pulled out a little wooden stool, and stood up upon it, and dipped a little piggin [pail] into the pitcher, and took out the full of it, and put it beside the stool, and then sat down under the pitcher, and began to work at putting a heel-piece on a bit of a brogue just fit for himself. "Well, by the powers," said Tom to himself, "I often heard tell of the Lepracauns, and, to tell God's truth, I never rightly believed in them—but here's one of them in real earnest. If I go knowingly to work, I'm a made man. They say a body must never take their eyes off them, or they'll escape."

Tom now stole on a little further, with his eye fixed on the little man just as a cat does with a mouse. So when he got up quite close to him, "God bless your work, neighbour," said Tom.

The little man raised up his head, and "Thank you kindly," said he.

"I wonder you'd be working on the holiday!" said Tom.

"That's my own business, not yours," was the reply.

"Well, may be you'd be civil enough to tell *us* what you've got in the pitcher there?" said Tom.

"That I will, with pleasure," said he; "it's good beer."

"Beer!" said Tom. "Thunder and fire! where did you get it?"

"Where did I get it, is it? Why, I made it. And what do you think I made it of?"

"Devil a one of me knows," said Tom; "but of malt, I suppose, what else?"

"There you're out. I made it of heath."

"Of heath!" said Tom, bursting out laughing; "sure you don't think me to be such a fool as to believe that?"

"Do as you please," said he, "but what I tell you is the truth. Did you never hear tell of the Danes."

"Well, what about *them?*" said Tom.

"Why, all the about them there is, is that when they were here they taught us to make beer out of the heath, and the secret's in my family ever since."

"Will you give a body a taste of your beer?" said Tom.

"I'll tell you what it is, young man, it would be fitter for you to be looking after your father's property than to be bothering decent quiet people with your foolish questions. There now, while you're idling away your time here, there's the cows have broke into the oats, and are knocking the corn all about."

Tom was taken so by surprise with this that he was just on the very point of turning round

when he recollected himself; so, afraid that
the like might happen again, he made a grab
at the Lepracaun, and caught him up in his
hand; but in his hurry he overset the pitcher,
and spilt all the beer, so that he could not get
a taste of it to tell what sort it was. He then
swore that he would kill him if he did not
show him where his money was. Tom looked
so wicked and so bloody-minded that the little man was quite frightened; so says he,
"Come along with me a couple of fields off,
and I'll show you a crock of gold."

So they went, and Tom held the Lepracaun
fast in his hand, and never took his eyes from
off him, though they had to cross hedges and
ditches, and a crooked bit of bog, till at last
they came to a great field all full of boliauns
[weeds], and the Lepracaun pointed to a big
boliaun, and says he, "Dig under that boliaun,
and you'll get the great crock all full of guineas."

Tom in his hurry had never thought of
bringing a spade with him, so he made up his
mind to run home and fetch one; and that he
might know the place again he took off one of
his red garters, and tied it round the boliaun.

Then he said to the Lepracaun, "Swear ye'll
not take that garter away from that boliaun."
And the Lepracaun swore right away not to
touch it.

"I suppose," said the Lepracaun, very civilly, "you have no further occasion for me?"

"No," says Tom; "you may go away now, if you please, and God speed you, and may good luck attend you wherever you go."

"Well, good-bye to you, Tom Fitzpatrick," said the Lepracaun; "and much good may it do you when you get it."

So Tom ran for dear life, till he came home and got a spade, and then away with him, as hard as he could go, back to the field of boliauns; but when he got there, lo and behold! not a boliaun in the field but had a red garter, the very model of his own, tied about it; and as to digging up the whole field, that was all nonsense, for there were more than forty good Irish acres in it. So Tom came home again with his spade on his shoulder, a little cooler than he went, and many's the hearty curse he gave the Lepracaun every time he thought of the neat turn he had served him.

Hudden and Dudden and
Donald O'Neary

THERE WAS ONCE upon a time two farmers, and their names were Hudden and Dudden. They had poultry in their yards, sheep on the uplands, and scores of cattle in the meadow-land alongside the river. But for all that they weren't happy. For just between their two farms there lived a poor man by the name of Donald O'Neary. He had a hovel over his head and a strip of grass that was barely enough to keep his one cow, Daisy, from starving, and, though she did her best, it was but seldom that Donald got a drink of milk or a roll of butter from Daisy. You would think there was little here to make Hudden and Dudden jealous, but so it is, the more one has the more one wants, and Donald's neighbours lay awake of nights scheming how they might get hold of his little strip of grass-land. Daisy, poor thing, they never thought of; she was just a bag of bones.

One day Hudden met Dudden, and they were soon grumbling as usual, and all to the tune of "If only we could get that vagabond Donald O'Neary out of the country."

"Let's kill Daisy," said Hudden at last; "if that doesn't make him clear out, nothing will."

No sooner said than agreed, and it wasn't dark before Hudden and Dudden crept up to the little shed where lay poor Daisy trying her best to chew the cud, though she hadn't had as much grass in the day as would cover your hand. And when Donald came to see if Daisy was all snug for the night, the poor beast had only time to lick his hand once before she died.

Well, Donald was a shrewd fellow, and down-hearted though he was, began to think if he could get any good out of Daisy's death. He thought and he thought, and the next day you could have seen him trudging off early to the fair, Daisy's hide over his shoulder, every penny he had jingling in his pockets. Just before he got to the fair, he made several slits in the hide, put a penny in each slit, walked into the best inn of the town as bold as if it belonged to him, and, hanging the hide up to a nail in the wall, sat down.

"Some of your best whisky," says he to the landlord. But the landlord didn't like his looks. "Is it fearing I won't pay you, you are?"

says Donald; "why I have a hide here that gives me all the money I want." And with that he hit it a whack with his stick and out hopped a penny. The landlord opened his eyes, as you may fancy.

"What'll you take for that hide?"

"It's not for sale, my good man."

"Will you take a gold piece?"

"It's not for sale, I tell you. Hasn't it kept me and mine for years?" and with that Donald hit the hide another whack and out jumped a second penny.

Well, the long and the short of it was that Donald let the hide go, and, that very evening, who but he should walk up to Hudden's door?

"Good-evening, Hudden. Will you lend me your best pair of scales?"

Hudden stared and Hudden scratched his head, but he lent the scales.

When Donald was safe at home, he pulled out his pocketful of bright gold and began to weigh each piece in the scales. But Hudden had put a lump of butter at the bottom, and so the last piece of gold stuck fast to the scales when he took them back to Hudden.

If Hudden had stared before, he stared ten times more now, and no sooner was Donald's back turned, than he was off as hard as he could pelt to Dudden's.

"Good-evening, Dudden. That vagabond, bad luck to him——"

"You mean Donald O'Neary?"

"And who else should I mean? He's back here weighing out sackfuls of gold."

"How do you know that?"

"Here are my scales that he borrowed, and here's a gold piece still sticking to them."

Off they went together, and they came to Donald's door. Donald had finished making the last pile of ten gold pieces. And he couldn't finish because a piece had stuck to the scales.

In they walked without an "If you please" or "By your leave."

"Well, *I* never!" that was all *they* could say.

"Good-evening, Hudden; good-evening, Dudden. Ah! you thought you had played me a fine trick, but you never did me a better turn in all your lives. When I found poor Daisy dead, I thought to myself, 'Well, her hide may fetch something;' and it did. Hides are worth their weight in gold in the market just now."

Hudden nudged Dudden, and Dudden winked at Hudden.

"Good-evening, Donald O'Neary."

"Good-evening, kind friends."

The next day there wasn't a cow or a calf that belonged to Hudden or Dudden but her hide was going to the fair in Hudden's biggest cart drawn by Dudden's strongest pair of horses.

When they came to the fair, each one took a hide over his arm, and there they were walking through the fair, bawling out at the top of their voices: "Hides to sell! hides to sell!"

Out came the tanner:

"How much for your hides, my good men?"

"Their weight in gold."

"It's early in the day to come out of the tavern." That was all the tanner said, and back he went to his yard.

"Hides to sell! Fine fresh hides to sell!"

Out came the cobbler.

"How much for your hides, my men?"

"Their weight in gold."

"Is it making game of me you are! Take that for your pains," and the cobbler dealt Hudden a blow that made him stagger.

Up the people came running from one end of the fair to the other. "What's the matter? What's the matter?" cried they.

"Here are a couple of vagabonds selling hides at their weight in gold," said the cobbler.

"Hold 'em fast; hold 'em fast!" bawled the innkeeper, who was the last to come up, he was so fat. "I'll wager it's one of the rogues who tricked me out of thirty gold pieces yesterday for a wretched hide."

It was more kicks than halfpence that Hudden and Dudden got before they were well on their way home again, and they didn't run the slower because all the dogs of the town were at their heels.

Well, as you may fancy, if they loved Donald little before, they loved him less now.

"What's the matter, friends?" said he, as he saw them tearing along, their hats knocked in, and their coats torn off, and their faces black and blue. "Is it fighting you've been? or mayhap you met the police, ill luck to them?"

"We'll police you, you vagabond. It's mighty smart you thought yourself, deluding us with your lying tales."

"Who deluded you? Didn't you see the gold with your own two eyes?"

But it was no use talking. Pay for it he must, and should. There was a meal-sack handy, and into it Hudden and Dudden popped Donald O'Neary, tied him up tight, ran a pole through the knot, and off they started for the Brown Lake of the Bog, each with a pole-end on his shoulder, and Donald O'Neary between.

But the Brown Lake was far, the road was dusty, Hudden and Dudden were sore and weary, and parched with thirst. There was an inn by the roadside.

"Let's go in," said Hudden; "I'm dead beat.

It's heavy he is for the little he had to eat."

If Hudden was willing, so was Dudden. As for Donald, you may be sure his leave wasn't asked, but he was lumped down at the inn door for all the world as if he had been a sack of potatoes.

"Sit still, you vagabond," said Dudden; "if we don't mind waiting, you needn't."

Donald held his peace, but after a while he heard the glasses clink, and Hudden singing away at the top of his voice.

"I won't have her, I tell you; I won't have her!" said Donald. But nobody heeded what he said.

"I won't have her, I tell you; I won't have her!" said Donald, and this time he said it louder; but nobody heeded what he said.

"I won't have her, I tell you; I won't have her!" said Donald; and this time he said it as loud as he could.

"And who won't you have, may I be so bold as to ask?" said a farmer, who had just come up with a drove of cattle, and was turning in for a glass.

"It's the king's daughter. They are bothering the life out of me to marry her."

"You're the lucky fellow. I'd give something to be in your shoes."

"Do you see that now! Wouldn't it be a fine

thing for a farmer to be marrying a princess, all dressed in gold and jewels?"

"Jewels, do you say? Ah, now, couldn't you take me with you?"

"Well, you're an honest fellow, and as I don't care for the king's daughter, though she's as beautiful as the day, and is covered with jewels from top to toe, you shall have her. Just undo the cord, and let me out; they tied me up tight, as they knew I'd run away from her."

Out crawled Donald; in crept the farmer.

"Now lie still, and don't mind the shaking; it's only rumbling over the palace steps you'll be. And maybe they'll abuse you for a vagabond, who won't have the king's daughter; but you needn't mind that. Ah! it's a deal I'm giving up for you, sure as it is that I don't care for the princess."

"Take my cattle in exchange," said the farmer; and you may guess it wasn't long before Donald was at their tails driving them homewards.

Out came Hudden and Dudden, and the one took one end of the pole, and the other the other.

"I'm thinking he's heavier," said Hudden.

"Ah, never mind," said Dudden; "it's only a step now to the Brown Lake.'

"I'll have her now! I'll have her now!" bawled the farmer, from inside the sack.

"By my faith, and you shall though," said Hudden, and he laid his stick across the sack.

"I'll have her! I'll have her!" bawled the farmer, louder than ever.

"Well, here you are," said Dudden, for they were now come to the Brown Lake, and, unslinging the sack, they pitched it plump into the lake.

"You'll not be playing your tricks on us any longer," said Hudden.

"True for you," said Dudden. "Ah, Donald, my boy, it was an ill day when you borrowed my scales."

Off they went, with a light step and an easy heart, but when they were near home, who should they see but Donald O'Neary, and all around him the cows were grazing, and the calves were kicking up their heels and butting their heads together.

"Is it you, Donald?" said Dudden. "Faith, you've been quicker than we have."

"True for you, Dudden, and let me thank you kindly; the turn was good, if the will was ill. You'll have heard, like me, that the Brown Lake leads to the Land of Promise. I always put it down as lies, but it is just as true as my word. Look at the cattle."

Hudden stared, and Dudden gaped; but they couldn't get over the cattle; fine fat cattle they were too.

"It's only the worst I could bring up with me," said Donald O'Neary; "the others were so fat, there was no driving them. Faith, too, it's little wonder they didn't care to leave, with grass as far as you could see, and as sweet and juicy as fresh butter."

"Ah, now, Donald, we haven't always been friends," said Dudden, "but, as I was just saying, you were ever a decent lad, and you'll show us the way, won't you?"

"I don't see that I'm called upon to do that; there is a power more cattle down there. Why shouldn't I have them all to myself?"

"Faith, they may well say, the richer you get, the harder the heart. You always were a neighbourly lad, Donald. You wouldn't wish to keep the luck all to yourself?"

"True for you, Hudden, though 'tis a bad example you set me. But I'll not be thinking of old times. There is plenty for all there, so come along with me."

Off they trudged, with a light heart and an eager step. When they came to the Brown Lake, the sky was full of little white clouds, and, if the sky was full, the lake was as full.

"Ah! now, look, there they are," cried Donald, as he pointed to the clouds in the lake.

"Where? where?" cried Hudden, and "Don't be greedy!" cried Dudden, as he jumped his hardest to be up first with the fat cattle. But if he jumped first, Hudden wasn't long behind.

They never came back. Maybe they got too fat, like the cattle. As for Donald O'Neary, he had cattle and sheep all his days to his heart's content.

The Old Hag's Long Leather Bag

ONCE ON A TIME, long, long ago, there was a widow woman who had three daughters. When their father died, their mother thought they never would want, for he had left her a long leather bag filled with gold and silver. But he was not long dead, when an old Hag came begging to the house one day and stole the long leather bag filled with gold and silver, and went away out of the country with it, no one knew where.

So from that day, the widow woman and her three daughters were poor, and she had a hard struggle to live and to bring up her three daughters.

But when they were grown up, the eldest said one day: "Mother, I'm a young woman now, and it's a shame for me to be here doing nothing to help you or myself. Bake me a bannock [flat bread] and cut me a callop [little cape], till I go away to push my fortune."

The mother baked her a whole bannock, and asked her if she would have half of it with her blessing or the whole of it without. She said to give her the whole bannock without.

So she took it and went away. She told them if she was not back in a year and a day from that, then they would know she was doing well, and making her fortune.

She traveled away and away before her, far further than I could tell you, and twice as far as you could tell me, until she came into a strange country, and going up to a little house, she found an old Hag living in it. The Hag asked her where she was going. She said she was going to push her fortune.

Said the Hag: "How would you like to stay here with me, for I want a maid?"

"What will I have to do?" said she.

"You will have to wash me and dress me, and sweep the hearth clean; but on the peril of your life, never look up the chimney," said the Hag.

"All right," she agreed to this.

The next day, when the Hag arose, she washed her and dressed her, and when the Hag went out, she swept the hearth clean, and she thought it would be no harm to have one wee look up the chimney. And there what did she see but her own mother's long leather bag of gold and silver? So she took it down at

"How would you like to stay here with me,
for I want a maid?"

once, and getting it on her back, started away for home as fast as she could run.

But she had not gone far when she met a horse grazing in a field, and when he saw her, he said: "Rub me! Rub me! for I haven't been rubbed these seven years."

But she only struck him with a stick she had in her hand, and drove him out of her way.

She had not gone much further when she met a sheep, who said: "O, shear me! Shear me! for I haven't been shorn these seven years."

But she struck the sheep, and sent it scurrying out of her way.

She had not gone much further when she met a goat tethered, and he said: "O, change my tether! Change my tether! for it hasn't been changed these seven years."

But she flung a stone at him, and went on.

Next she came to a lime-kiln, and it said: "O, clean me! Clean me! for I haven't been cleaned these seven years."

But she only scowled at it, and hurried on.

After another bit she met a cow, and it said: "O, milk me! Milk me! for I haven't been milked these seven years."

She struck the cow out of her way, and went on.

Then she came to a mill. The mill said: "O, turn me! Turn me! for I haven't been turned these seven years."

But she did not heed what it said, only went in and lay down behind the mill door, with the bag under her head, for it was then night.

When the hag came into her hut again and found the girl gone, she ran to the chimney and looked up to see if she had carried off the bag. She got into a great rage, and she started to run as fast as she could after her.

She had not gone far when she met the horse, and she said: "O, horse, horse of mine, did you see this maid of mine, with my tig, with my tag, with my long leather bag, and all the gold and silver I have earned since I was a maid?"

"Ay," said the horse, "it is not long since she passed here."

So on she ran, and it was not long till she met the sheep, and said she: "Sheep, sheep of mine, did you see this maid of mine, with my tig, with my tag, with my long leather bag, and all the gold and silver I have earned since I was a maid?"

"Ay," said the sheep, "it is not long since she passed here."

So she goes on, and it was not long before she met the goat, and said she: "Goat, goat of mine, did you see this maid of mine, with my tig, with my tag, with my long leather bag, and all the gold and silver I have earned since I was a maid?"

"Ay," said the goat, "it is not long since she passed here."

So she goes on, and it was not long before she met the lime-kiln, and said she: "Lime-kiln, lime-kiln of mine, did you see this maid of mine, with my tig, with my tag, with my long leather bag, and with all the gold and silver I have earned since I was a maid?"

"Ay," said the lime-kiln, "it is not long since she passed here."

So she goes on, and it was not long before she met the cow, and said she, "Cow, cow of mine, did you see this maid of mine, with my tig, with my tag, with my long leather bag, and all the gold and silver I have earned since I was a maid?"

"Ay," said the cow, "it is not long since she passed here."

So she goes on, and it was not long before she met the mill, and said she: "Mill, mill of mine, did you see this maid of mine, with my tig, with my tag, with my long leather bag, and all the gold and silver I have earned since I was a maid?"

And the mill said: "Yes, she is sleeping behind the door."

She went in and struck her with a white rod, and turned her into a stone. She then took the bag of gold and silver on her back, and went away back home.

A year and a day had gone by after the eldest daughter left home, and when they found she had not returned, the second daughter got up, and she said: "My sister must be doing well and making her fortune, and isn't it a shame for me to be sitting here doing nothing, either to help you, mother, or myself. Bake me a bannock," said she, "and cut me a callop, till I go away to push my fortune."

The mother did this, and asked her would she have half the bannock with her blessing or the whole bannock without.

She said the whole bannock without, and she set off. Then she said: "If I am not back here in a year and a day, you may be sure that I am doing well and making my fortune," and then she went away.

She traveled away and away on before her, far further than I could tell you, and twice as far as you could tell me, until she came into a strange country, and going up to a little house, she found an old Hag living in it. The old Hag asked her where she was going. She said she was going to push her fortune.

Said the Hag: "How would you like to stay here with me, for I want a maid?"

"What will I have to do?" says she.

"You'll have to wash me and dress me, and sweep the hearth clean; and on the peril of your life never look up the chimney," said the Hag.

"All right," she agreed to this.

The next day, when the Hag arose, she washed her and dressed her, and when the Hag went out she swept the hearth, and she thought it would be no harm to have one wee look up the chimney. And there what did she see but her own mother's long leather bag of gold and silver? So she took it down at once, and getting it on her back, started away for home as fast as she could run.

But she had not gone far when she met a horse grazing in a field, and when he saw her, he said: "Rub me! Rub me! for I haven't been rubbed these seven years."

But she only struck him with a stick she had in her hand, and drove him out of her way.

She had not gone much further when she met the sheep, who said: "O, shear me! Shear me! for I haven't been shorn in seven years."

But she struck the sheep, and sent it scurrying out of her way.

She had not gone much further when she met the goat tethered, and he said: "O, change my tether! Change my tether! for it hasn't been changed in seven years."

But she flung a stone at him, and went on.

Next she came to the lime-kiln, and that said: "O, clean me! Clean me! for I haven't been cleaned these seven years."

But she only scowled at it, and hurried on.

Then she came to the cow, and it said: "O, milk me! Milk me! for I haven't been milked these seven years."

She struck the cow out of her way, and went on.

Then she came to the mill. The mill said: "O, turn me! Turn me! for I haven't been turned these seven years."

But she did not heed what it said, only went in and lay down behind the mill door, with the bag under her head, for it was then night.

When the Hag came into her hut again and found the girl gone, she ran to the chimney and looked up to see if she had carried off the bag. She got into a great rage, and she started to run as fast as she could after her.

She had not gone far when she met the horse, and she said: "O, horse, horse of mine, did you see this maid of mine, with my tig, with my tag, with my long leather bag, and all the gold and silver I have earned since I was a maid?"

"Ay," said the horse, "it is not long since she passed here."

So on she ran, and it was not long until she met the sheep, and said she: "Oh, sheep, sheep of mine, did you see this maid of mine, with my tig, with my tag, with my long leather bag, and all the gold and silver I have earned since I was a maid?"

"Ay," said the sheep, "it is not long since she passed here."

So she goes on, and it was not long before she met the goat, and said: "Goat, goat of mine, did you see this maid of mine, with my tig, with my tag, with my long leather bag, and all the gold and silver I have earned since I was a maid?"

"Ay," said the goat, "it is not long since she passed here."

So she goes on, and it was not long before she met the lime-kiln, and said she: "Lime-kiln, lime-kiln of mine, did you see this maid of mine, with my tig, with my tag, with my long leather bag, and all the gold and silver I have earned since I was a maid?"

"Ay," said the lime-kiln, "it is not long since she passed here."

So she goes on, and it was not long before she met the cow, and says she: "Cow, cow of mine, did you see this maid of mine, with my tig, with my tag, with my long leather bag, and all the gold and silver I have earned since I was a maid?"

"Ay," said the cow, "it is not long since she passed here."

So she goes on, and it was not long before she met the mill, and said she: "Mill, mill of mine, did you see this maid of mine, with my tig, with my tag, with my long leather bag, and all the gold and silver I have earned since I was a maid?"

And the mill said: "Yes, she is sleeping behind the door."

She went in and struck her with a white rod, and turned her into a stone. She then took the bag of gold and silver on her back and went home.

When the second daughter had been gone a year and a day and she hadn't come back, the youngest daughter said: "My two sisters must be doing very well indeed, and making great fortunes when they are not coming back, and it's a shame for me to be sitting here doing nothing, either to help you, mother, or myself. Make me a bannock and cut me a callop, till I go away and push my fortune."

The mother did this and asked her would she have half of the bannock with her blessing or the whole bannock without.

She said: "I will have half of the bannock with your blessing, mother."

The mother gave her a blessing and half a bannock, and she set out.

She traveled away and away on before her, far further than I could tell you, and twice as far as you could tell me, until she came into a strange country, and going up to a little house, she found an old Hag living in it. The Hag asked her where she was going. She said she was going to push her fortune.

Said the Hag: "How would you like to stay here with me, for I want a maid?"

"What will I have to do?" said she.

"You'll have to wash me and dress me, and sweep the hearth clean; and on the peril of your life never look up the chimney," said the Hag.

"All right," she agreed to this.

The next day when the Hag arose, she washed her and dressed her, and when the Hag went out she swept the hearth, and she thought it would be no harm to have one wee look up the chimney, and there what did she see but her own mother's long leather bag of gold and silver? So she took it down at once, and getting it on her back, started away for home as fast as she could run.

When she got to the horse, the horse said:

"Rub me! Rub me! for I haven't been rubbed these seven years."

"Oh, poor horse, poor horse," she said, "I'll surely do that." And she laid down her bag, and rubbed the horse.

Then she went on, and it wasn't long before she met the sheep, who said: "Oh, shear me, shear me! for I haven't been shorn these seven years."

"O, poor sheep, poor sheep," she said, "I'll surely do that," and she laid down the bag, and sheared the sheep.

On she went till she met the goat, who said: "O, change my tether! Change my tether! for it hasn't been changed these seven years."

"O, poor goat, poor goat," she said, "I'll surely do that," and she laid down the bag, and changed the goat's tether.

Then she went on till she met the lime-kiln. The lime-kiln said: "O, clean me! Clean me! for I haven't been cleaned these seven years."

"O, poor lime-kiln, poor lime-kiln," she said, "I'll surely do that," and she laid down the bag and cleaned the lime-kiln.

Then she went on and met the cow. The cow said: "O, milk me! Milk me! for I haven't been milked these seven years."

"O, poor cow, poor cow," she said, "I'll

surely do that," and she laid down the bag and milked the cow.

At last she reached the mill. The mill said: "O, turn me! turn me! for I haven't been turned these seven years."

"O, poor mill, poor mill," she said, "I'll surely do that," and she turned the mill too.

As night was on her, she went in and lay down behind the mill door to sleep.

When the Hag came into her hut again and found the girl gone, she ran to the chimney to see if she had carried off the bag. She got into a great rage, and started to run as fast as she could after her.

She had not gone far until she came up to the horse and said: "O, horse, horse of mine, did you see this maid of mine, with my tig, with my tag, with my long leather bag, and all the gold and silver I have earned since I was a maid?"

The horse said: "Do you think I have nothing to do only watch your maids for you? You may go somewhere else and look for information."

Then she came upon the sheep. "O, sheep, sheep of mine, have you seen this maid of mine, with my tig, with my tag, with my long leather bag, and all the gold and silver I have earned since I was a maid?"

The sheep said: "Do you think I have nothing to do only watch your maids for you? You may go somewhere else and look for information."

Then she went on till she met the goat. "O, goat, goat of mine, have you seen this maid of mine, with my tig, with my tag, with my long leather bag, and all the gold and silver I have earned since I was a maid?"

The goat said: "Do you think I have nothing to do only watch your maids for you? You can go somewhere else and look for information."

Then she went on till she came to the lime-kiln. "O, lime-kiln, lime-kiln of mine, did you see this maid of mine, with my tig, with my tag, with my long leather bag, and all the gold and silver I have earned since I was a maid?"

Said the lime-kiln: "Do you think I have nothing to do only to watch your maids for you? You may go somewhere else and look for information."

Next she met the cow. "O, cow, cow of mine, have you seen this maid of mine, with my tig, with my tag, with my long leather bag, and all the gold and silver I have earned since I was a maid?"

The cow said: "Do you think I have nothing to do only watch your maids for you? You may go somewhere else and look for information."

Then she got to the mill. "O, mill, mill of mine, have you seen this maid of mine, with my tig, with my tag, with my long leather bag, and all the gold and silver I have earned since I was a maid?"

The mill said: "Come nearer and whisper to me."

She went nearer to whisper to the mill, and the mill dragged her under the wheels and ground her up.

The old Hag had dropped the white rod out of her hand, and the mill told the young girl to take this white rod and strike two stones behind the mill door. She did that, and her two sisters stood up. She hoisted the leather bag on her back, and the three of them set out and traveled away and away till they reached home.

The mother had been crying all the time while they were away, and was now ever so glad to see them, and rich and happy they all lived ever after.

The Giant's Stairs

ON THE ROAD between Passage and Cork there is an old mansion called Ronayne's Court. It may be easily known from the stack of chimneys and the gable ends, which are to be seen look at it which way you will. Here it was that Maurice Ronayne and his wife Margaret Gould kept house, as may be learned to this day from the great old chimneypiece, on which is carved their arms. They were a mighty worthy couple, and had but one son, who was called Philip, after no less a person than the King of Spain.

Immediately on his smelling the cold air of this world the child sneezed, which was naturally taken to be a good sign of his having a clear head; and the subsequent rapidity of his learning was truly amazing, for on the very first day a primer was put into his hands he tore out the A, B, C page and destroyed it, as a thing quite beneath his notice. No wonder then that both father and mother were proud of their heir, who gave such indisputable proofs of genius, or, as they called it in that part of the world, "*genus.*"

One morning, however, Master Phil, who was then just seven years old, was missing, and no one could tell what had become of him: servants were sent in all directions to seek him, on horseback and on foot, but they returned without any tidings of the boy, whose disappearance altogether was most unaccountable. A large reward was offered, but it produced them no intelligence, and years rolled away without Mr. and Mrs. Ronayne having obtained any satisfactory account of the fate of their lost child.

There lived at this time, near Carrigaline, one Robert Kelly, a blacksmith by trade. He was what is termed a handy man, and his abilities were held in much estimation by the lads and the lasses of the neighbourhood; for, independent of shoeing horses, which he did to great perfection, and making plough-irons, he interpreted dreams for the young women, sung Arthur O'Bradley at their weddings, and was so good-natured a fellow at a christening, that he was gossip [godfather] to half the country round.

Now it happened that Robin had a dream himself, and young Philip Ronayne appeared to him in it, at the dead hour of the night. Robin thought he saw the boy mounted upon a beautiful white horse, and that he told him how he was made a page to the giant Mahon Mac Mahon, who had carried him off, and who held his court in the hard heart of the rock. "The seven years—my time of service— are clean out, Robin," said he, "and if you release me this night I will be the making of you for ever after."

"And how will I know," said Robin— cunning enough, even in his sleep—"but this is all a dream?"

"Take that," said the boy, "for a token"—and at the word the white horse struck out with one of his hind legs, and gave poor Robin such a kick in the forehead that, thinking he was a dead man, he roared as loud as he could after his brains, and woke up calling a thousand murders. He found himself in bed, but he had the mark of the blow, the regular print of a horse-shoe upon his forehead as red as blood; and Robin Kelly, who never before found himself puzzled at the dream of any other person, did not know what to think of his own.

Robin was well acquainted with the Giant's Stairs—as, indeed, who is not that knows the harbour? They consist of great masses of rock, which, piled one above another, rise like

a flight of steps from very deep water, against
the bold cliff of Carrigmahon. Nor are they
badly suited for stairs to those who have legs
of sufficient length to stride over a moderate-
sized house, or to enable them to clear the
space of a mile in a hop, step, and jump. Both
these feats the giant Mac Mahon was said to
have performed in the days of Finnian glory;[1]
and the common tradition of the country
placed his dwelling within the cliff up whose
side the stairs led.

Such was the impression which the dream
made on Robin, that he determined to put its
truth to the test. It occurred to him, however,
before setting out on this adventure, that a
plough-iron may be no bad companion, as,
from experience, he knew it was an excellent
knock-down argument, having on more occa-
sions than one settled a little disagreement
very quietly: so, putting one on his shoulder,
off he marched, in the cool of the evening,
through Glaun a Thowk (the Hawk's Glen) to
Monkstown. Here an old gossip of his (Tom
Clancey by name) lived, who, on hearing Robin's dream, promised him the use of his skiff,
and moreover offered to assist in rowing it to
the Giant's Stairs.

After a supper which was of the best, they
embarked. It was a beautiful still night, and

[1] The legendary days of the hero Finn Mac Cool.

the little boat glided swiftly along. The regular
dip of the oars, the distant song of the sailor,
and sometimes the voice of a belated traveller
at the ferry of Carrigaloe, alone broke the qui-
etness of the land and sea and sky. The tide
was in their favour, and in a few minutes
Robin and his gossip rested on their oars
under the dark shadow of the Giant's Stairs.
Robin looked anxiously for the entrance to
the Giant's palace, which, it was said, may be
found by any one seeking it at midnight; but
no such entrance could he see. His impatience
had hurried him there before that time, and
after waiting a considerable space in a state
of suspense not to be described, Robin, with
pure vexation, could not help exclaiming to
his companion, "'Tis a pair of fools we are,
Tom Clancey, for coming here at all on the
strength of a dream."

"And whose doing is it," said Tom, "but your
own?"

At the moment he spoke they perceived a
faint glimmering of light to proceed from the
cliff, which gradually increased until a porch
big enough for a king's palace unfolded itself
almost on a level with the water. They pulled
the skiff directly towards the opening, and
Robin Kelly, seizing his plough-iron, boldly
entered with a strong hand and a stout heart.

Wild and strange was that entrance.

Wild and strange was that entrance; the whole
of which appeared formed of grim and gro-
tesque faces, blending so strangely each with
the other that it was impossible to define any:
the chin of one formed the nose of another;
what appeared to be a fixed and stern eye, if
dwelt upon, changed to a gaping mouth; and
the lines of the lofty forehead grew into a
majestic and flowing beard. The more Robin
allowed himself to contemplate the forms
around him, the more terrific they became;
and the stony expression of this crowd of
faces assumed a savage ferocity as his imagi-
nation converted feature after feature into a
different shape and character. Losing the twi-
light in which these indefinite forms were visi-
ble, he advanced through a dark and devious
passage, whilst a deep and rumbling noise
sounded as if the rock was about to close
upon him and swallow him up alive for ever.
Now, indeed, poor Robin felt afraid.

"Robin, Robin," said he, "if you were a fool
for coming here, what in the name of fortune
are you now?" But, as before, he had scarcely
spoken, when he saw a small light twinkling
through the darkness of the distance, like a
star in the midnight sky. To retreat was out of
the question; for so many turnings and wind-

ings were in the passage, that he considered
he had but little chance of making his way
back. He therefore proceeded towards the bit
of light, and came at last into a spacious
chamber, from the roof of which hung the sol-
itary lamp that had guided him. Emerging
from such profound gloom, the single lamp
afforded Robin abundant light to discover
several gigantic figures seated round a mas-
sive stone table, as if in serious deliberation,
but no word disturbed the breathless silence
which prevailed. At the head of this table sat
Mahon Mac Mahon himself, whose majestic
beard had taken root and in the course of
ages grown into the stone slab. He was the
first who perceived Robin; and instantly start-
ing up, drew his long beard from out the huge
piece of rock in such haste and with so sudden a jerk that it was shattered into a thousand pieces.

"What seek you?" he demanded in a voice
of thunder.

"I come," answered Robin, with as much
boldness as he could put on, for his heart was
almost fainting within him; "I come," said he,
"to claim Philip Ronayne, whose time of service is out this night."

"And who sent you here?" said the giant.

"'Twas of my own accord I came," said
Robin.

"Then you must single him out from among my pages," said the giant; "and if you fix on the wrong one, your life is the forfeit. Follow me." He led Robin into a hall of vast extent, and filled with lights; along either side of which were rows of beautiful children, all apparently seven years old, and none beyond that age, dressed in green, and every one exactly dressed alike.

"Here," said Mahon, "you are free to take Philip Ronayne, if you will; but, remember, I give but one choice."

Robin was sadly perplexed; for there were hundreds upon hundreds of children; and he had no very clear recollection of the boy he sought. But he walked along the hall, by the side of Mahon, as if nothing was the matter, although his great iron dress clanked fearfully at every step, sounding louder than Robin's own sledge battering on his anvil.

They had nearly reached the end without speaking, when Robin, seeing that the only means he had was to make friends with the giant, determined to try what effect a few soft words might have.

"'Tis a fine wholesome appearance the poor children carry," remarked Robin, "although they have been here so long shut out from the fresh air and the blessed light of heaven. 'Tis tenderly your honour must have reared them!"

"Ay," said the giant, "that is true for you; so give me your hand; for you are, I believe, a very honest fellow for a blacksmith."

Robin at the first look did not much like the huge size of the hand, and therefore presented his plough-iron, which the giant seizing, twisted in his grasp round and round again as if it had been a potato stalk; on seeing this all the children set up a shout of laughter. In the midst of their mirth Robin thought he heard his name called; and all ear and eye, he put his hand on the boy who he fancied had spoken, crying out at the same time, "Let me live or die for it, but this is young Phil Ronayne."

"It is Philip Ronayne—happy Philip Ronayne," said his young companions; and in an instant the hall became dark. Crashing noises were heard, and all was in strange confusion; but Robin held fast his prize, and found himself lying in the grey dawn of the morning at the head of the Giant's Stairs with the boy clasped in his arms.

Robin had plenty of gossips to spread the story of his wonderful adventure: Passage, Monkstown, Carrigaline—the whole barony of Kerricurrihy rung with it.

"Are you quite sure, Robin, it is young Phil Ronayne you have brought back with you?"

was the regular question; for although the boy had been seven years away, his appearance now was just the same as on the day he was missed. He had neither grown taller nor older in look, and he spoke of things which had happened before he was carried off as one awakened from sleep, or as if they had occurred yesterday.

"Am I sure? Well, that's a queer question," was Robin's reply; "seeing the boy has the blue eye of the mother, with the foxy hair of the father; to say nothing of the *purty* wart on the right side of his little nose."

However Robin Kelly may have been questioned, the worthy couple of Ronayne's Court doubted not that he was the deliverer of their child from the power of the giant Mac Mahon; and the reward they bestowed on him equalled their gratitude.

Philip Ronayne lived to be an old man; and he was remarkable to the day of his death for his skill in working brass and iron, which it was believed he had learned during his seven years' apprenticeship to the giant Mahon Mac Mahon.

DOVER CHILDREN'S THRIFT CLASSICS

Just $1.00

All books complete and unabridged, except where noted.
96pp., 5³⁄₁₆″ × 8¹⁄₄″, paperbound.

AESOP'S FABLES, Aesop. 28020-9

THE LITTLE MERMAID AND OTHER FAIRY TALES, Hans Christian Andersen. 27816-6

THE UGLY DUCKLING AND OTHER FAIRY TALES, Hans Christian Andersen. 27081-5

THE THREE BILLY GOATS GRUFF AND OTHER READ-ALOUD STORIES, Carolyn Sherwin Bailey (ed.). 28021-7

THE STORY OF PETER PAN, James M. Barrie and Daniel O'Connor. 27294-X

ROBIN HOOD, Bob Blaisdell. 27573-6

THE ADVENTURES OF BUSTER BEAR, Thornton W. Burgess. 27564-7

THE ADVENTURES OF CHATTERER THE RED SQUIRREL, Thornton W. Burgess. 27399-7

THE ADVENTURES OF DANNY MEADOW MOUSE, Thornton W. Burgess. 27565-5

THE ADVENTURES OF GRANDFATHER FROG, Thornton W. Burgess. 27400-4

THE ADVENTURES OF JERRY MUSKRAT, Thornton W. Burgess. 27817-4

THE ADVENTURES OF JIMMY SKUNK, Thornton W. Burgess. 28023-3

THE ADVENTURES OF PETER COTTONTAIL, Thornton W. Burgess. 26929-9

THE ADVENTURES OF POOR MRS. QUACK, Thornton W. Burgess. 27818-2

THE ADVENTURES OF REDDY FOX, Thornton W. Burgess. 26930-2

THE SECRET GARDEN, Frances Hodgson Burnett. (abridged) 28024-1

PICTURE FOLK-TALES, Valery Carrick. 27083-1

THE STORY OF POCAHONTAS, Brian Doherty (ed.). 28025-X

SLEEPING BEAUTY AND OTHER FAIRY TALES, Jacob and Wilhelm Grimm. 27084-X

THE ELEPHANT'S CHILD AND OTHER JUST SO STORIES, Rudyard Kipling. 27821-2

HOW THE LEOPARD GOT HIS SPOTS AND OTHER JUST SO STORIES, Rudyard Kipling. 27297-4

MOWGLI STORIES FROM "THE JUNGLE BOOK," Rudyard Kipling. 28030-6

NONSENSE POEMS, Edward Lear. 28031-4

BEAUTY AND THE BEAST AND OTHER FAIRY TALES, Marie Leprince de Beaumont and Charles Perrault. 28032-2

A DOG OF FLANDERS, Ouida (Marie Louise de la Ramée). 27087-4

PETER RABBIT AND 11 OTHER FAVORITE TALES, Beatrix Potter. 27845-X